Praise for Deidre Knight's
Parallel Fire

"Deidre Knight has written a love story that is short and much more then sweet. Parallel Fire is a joy to read, and a great treat, especially for fans of the Midnight Warrior series."

~ *Fallen Angel Reviews*

"Don't miss this passionate story; it's a sure winner!"

~ *Romance Reviews Today*

"Parallel Fire is a sexy, entertaining romance set in an exotic paranormal world."

~ *The Romance Studio*

"I liked Parallel Fire very much. ...Parallel Fire is worth reading – I should know. I've read it twice!"

~ *Joyfully Reviewed*

Look for these titles by
Deidre Knight

Now Available:

Butterfly Tattoo

Parallel Fire

A Midnight Warriors book

Deidre Knight

A SAMHAIN PUBLISHING, LTD. publication.

Samhain Publishing, Ltd.
577 Mulberry Street, Suite 1520
Macon, GA 31201
www.samhainpublishing.com

Parallel Fire
Copyright © 2010 by Deidre Knight
Print ISBN: 978-1-60928-135-9
Digital ISBN: 978-1-60504-039-4

Editing by Tera Kleinfelter
Cover by Natalie Winters

First Samhain Publishing, Ltd. electronic publication: June 2008
First Samhain Publishing, Ltd. print publication: August 2010

Dedication

To a true warrior in my life, someone whose strength inspires me daily—my sister, Pamela Harty.

And to a sexy man who I'd gladly be marooned with in the wilderness *any day*—my husband, Judson Knight.

I love you both very much!

Prologue

Every face in the meeting room was turned toward her, every leader, every lieutenant staring at Anna in cool appraisal. She sucked in a steadying breath as the meeting room doors were closed behind them, and came to attention in front of Lieutenant Nevin Daniels, giving him a crisp salute that he returned. After seventeen years as part of her king's most elite band of royal protectors, the Madjin Circle, it seemed almost impossible to believe that she was on trial before their top security advisor.

Well, it wasn't precisely a trial, not really—her king had forgiven her deception, as well as that of the other protectors who had been fighting in their king, Jared Bennett's, midst, never revealing their true identities to him. She'd hated that secretive existence, but she'd been pledged and branded as a royal protector at the tender age of twelve; that meant you obeyed your Madjin unit leader implicitly, didn't ask questions. You followed directives in order to protect your king and commander— even without his knowing, if need be.

Oh, yes, her king's advisors expected debriefing; they anticipated answers and revelations. With a glance across the table before her, she wondered how this meeting would go, with her in the proverbial hot seat. There were too many people gathered; too much pressure rode on this single moment. If only the long table weren't populated with so many of those from their top leadership.

Nevin Daniels, the highest-ranking officer in the room—the fourth within their overall command, to be exact—glanced down at an open dossier spread on the table before him, and without looking up said, "At ease, Lieutenant."

She released a tense breath, one that she hadn't even realized she'd been holding.

"You know why you're here before us today, correct?" Daniels continued.

"Yes, sir. To describe the activities of the Madjin, and in particular my role within the Circle."

"Very well." He closed the folder, glancing upward. "Let's begin."

And so it was that Anna found herself staring into the darkest, most arresting pair of Refarian eyes that she had ever seen. Eyes she'd known for much of her life; ones that belonged to a man who was her chief interrogator this day.

Lieutenant Nevin Daniels had first come to the palace back on Refaria when she was only a girl. Powerful, absolutely radiating authority and privilege, he wasn't exactly the sort who put you at ease. Because he and Anna lived in the same lodge, ate at the same table, served beside one another daily here in the Wyoming compound...well, his untouchable beauty had always left her edgy and uncomfortable.

"Lieutenant," he started calmly, a semi-scowl on his face, "please explain the details of your initiation into the Madjin Circle."

Nevin kept talking, but she couldn't seem to hear a word he said. And it was completely his fault, no question about it. Those ridiculously long-lashed eyes of his, the swarthy skin that contrasted exotically with the silver in his hair, the high cheekbones—the man's looks were enough to distract even the toughest of female soldiers.

Pressing her eyes shut, she took a deep breath and began. "I was tapped for the Madjin when I was a little girl. My mother and father were part of the Circle, my grandparents before them, and on back up the line."

"A family inheritance," Daniels noted thoughtfully.

She couldn't help but smile with pride. "Always."

One of the under-lieutenants transcribed the interview into his handheld, working feverishly to capture her answers.

"How old, Lieutenant?" Nevin reviewed some notes on his own handheld. "I am told that six is the first age for a Madjin to enter the service?"

"It varies, sir—but we are given the brand at twelve."

"The brand?" His left eyebrow lifted a millimeter.

"Right here." She tapped the inside of her wrist. "It's an energized tattoo."

"Hidden?" His voice assumed a slightly husky sound,

as if her invisible Madjin emblem were something dangerous and sexy. As if the very thought of her revealing it to him were an automatic turn-on.

Yet when she looked up, he seemed perfectly composed.

I'd just love to get this guy to fall apart at my hands. To make him scream my name and show me what he's really made of. A flush crept down her cheeks and into her neck.

For a split second, Nevin's black eyebrows quirked together. "Are you all right, Lieutenant Draekus?"

Gods, he must be able to see how I'm blushing. She swallowed, suppressing a smile. "More than fine, sir."

"Very well, may I see this mark of the Madjin, then?"

Her blush intensified. "See my mark?" she almost squeaked, glancing anxiously at the roomful of advisors and officers. Nevin tracked with her, noting the eight others sitting around him.

He leaned back into his chair, appraising her. His gaze lingered for a long moment on her flushed face. "That is what would be expected, would it not?"

With one more sweep about the room, she bowed her head. "It's...personal. Deeply personal."

"But if it cannot verify your claim, then what is the point of the mark?"

She chewed on her lip, staring at the polished hardwood flooring between them. "I will show my king, but no one else."

"You aren't willing to reveal it to me." It was a statement of fact, edged with the slightest hint of anger. But then he lifted a hand, issued several quiet commands, and the other lieutenants and advisors at the table stood, preparing to make their exit. Nevin nodded to several of the departing officers, and only once the door had closed quietly on the two of them, did he return his gaze to hers.

"Now you will show this mark of the Madjin to me."

She hesitated a moment, then stepped closer, placed both hands on the edge of the table that separated them, and leaned toward him. "It's my energy, sir. It's more than just a mark...it's my *energy*. Surely you understand how personal that is."

Without meaning to, she made a small cry of frustration and embarrassment, and Daniels jolted visibly at the quiet sound. This time, the advisor's own dark cheeks reddened slightly, and he shifted in his chair. He gave a stern, considering nod. "Very well. We will arrange for a meeting with the commander."

"Thank you, sir." She exhaled in relief, and for a split-second their gazes locked, and she swore—damn it, it had to be—that the unflappable, stoic lieutenant smiled suggestively at her. Just a hint of the way his mouth tilted sideways, something about how his thick-lashed eyes lowered almost imperceptibly.

"One's energy can, of course, be quite personal," he agreed, "although it depends on the individual." His keen black eyes narrowed, danger glittering in their depths.

"You strike me as a woman with a very powerful, intense...amount of it."

Anna's mouth fell slack, the burning in her face spread to every extremity, and she stumbled a step backward. Why would Daniels have chosen this particular instance to dismantle every bit of her self-composure and pride when it came to interacting with him? Was it some sort of strategy or maneuver intended to fluster her and thereby learn Madjin secrets?

"You strike me the same way, sir," she fired off without thinking—and only when the words were out of her mouth did she realize that she'd just flirted with her commanding officer. "I mean, I'm just saying, that...well, you have so much power. Personal power. Energy—"

"Anna, I understand." Nevin shocked her by laughing softly, a slow rumbling sound that began deep within his chest. She had never—not once in the past six years of living in the compound with the lieutenant—heard him laugh. "I understand, and you certainly flatter a man like me, so obviously in his maturity."

All Refarian males entered their maturity by their mid-forties, some quite a bit earlier. It was the time when they could no longer sire children—a transformation that came for the *male* Refarians, not the females—and was said to be marked by intense sexual compulsions and drives.

"Sir, you may have matured, but"—she hesitated, grasping for the right words—"you still seem perfectly virile to me."

"Virile." His eyes sparkled mischievously. "For a mature man, that's quite the way to put it."

"You're still very young. Not even forty, right?"

He shot her a cocky glance. "Thirty-eight next month."

"Then virile should be the perfect word."

He laughed faintly. "Except, as it seems, when it comes to siring children."

"But the rumors, sir...they all indicate that mature men are—"

He raised a confident hand, silencing her. "Please, Lieutenant Draekus."

Oh, gods above, she swore inwardly, *what was I thinking?* To have discussed her commanding officer's sexuality—his life change—even his potential prowess in bed? And at a moment when she should have been showing more respect than usual? Damn, she was losing it for real.

Draping his arm over the chair beside him, he regarded her for a long moment. She noticed that his breathing seemed to have increased slightly, and felt her own pulse skitter to a crazy hyper-drive tempo. "I like a soldier who speaks her mind plainly." His moody eyes narrowed. "I have always admired this about you, Anna Draekus."

She inclined her head. "Thank you, sir. I'm sorry, sir, if I offended you in any way. I don't know what got into me; please just forgive me for any disrespect—"

"Look at me, Anna," he half-whispered, and she

managed—somehow—to meet his gaze.

He leaned forward in his chair, his breathing slightly heavy. Suddenly, the man staring back at her seemed completely at odds with the intense, reserved one she'd been serving underneath for so long. This Nevin Daniels didn't seem unknowable or cool—he seemed as sensuous and dangerous as she'd just suggested he might be. He opened his mouth, about to say something, but then closed it, glancing away from her.

When he looked at her again, the devouring, seductive look had faded from his voice and expression—vanished like a whisper on the Wyoming wind. "Shall you enlighten us as to your role back on Refaria?" he continued, as if nothing had just transpired between the two of them. Just like that, and the interview resumed. No more flirtatious look, no more half-glimpse of the sun. Only cool, officious Lieutenant Nevin Daniels staring back at her.

And she'd be damned if she wouldn't find her way behind that rigid self-composure of his once again.

Nevin stared into the mirror of the athletic facility, dripping with sweat. After his interview with Lieutenant Draekus he'd been infused with so much heat and lust, he'd hit the workout area in an effort to expend at least some percentage of that roiling need. Routinely, he did everything in his power to avoid her: Ate at the opposite end of the dining table from her, passed by the recreation area if he observed her in it. Only on rare occasions were they forced to work together, and without fail he never had a word to say to the woman; he was always tied in knots, unable to find a way to tease or flirt or even speak with her. And without fail, those interactions always left him wound this tight, as if his body were a sensual volcano that only she controlled.

Of course, his first breakthrough would have happened in the meeting chamber, he thought ruefully, as he toweled off his bare chest, then his silver hair. His face was flushed from running; he'd just spent an hour and a half on the track that looped the top side of the hangar, sprinting for at least half of that time. Friday night meant that the place had been emptied, and so he'd pushed himself to the very limit, every step meant to exorcise Anna Drackus from his thoughts and body once and for all.

Nothing *ever* worked.

And she had absolutely no idea that he'd spent years near her, totally infatuated beyond reason. What an embarrassment for one of the king's highest advisors; he was hardly better than a fledgling entering his first season—and gods knew he was old enough to know better. Plenty old enough.

Disgusted with his paralyzing inaction, he'd finally resolved to make a move on her early last year—but had entered his maturity unexpectedly. That first morning, gazing at his newly silvering hair, he'd known he could never make a suitable mate, not for someone as young and vivacious as Anna. He was only thirty-seven then,

17

entering his change far earlier than was usual for the male of their species, but she had to be a decade younger than he, at the very least. That kind of age gap—and his inability to prove a proper mate—well, it had been enough to cause him to forget any plans of taking action with Anna.

Of course, here it was almost a year later, and he wasn't so sure he'd made the right choice after all. His sexuality churned within him daily, driving him harder and harder, practically to the brink of insanity. Without a partner or mate, he had no outlet for channeling the intense sexual transformation within his Refarian body. What he needed was to bond, to take a lifemate who would accept his dizzying physical lusts. The question was how could he ever approach Anna now that so many years had drifted past them both? He hardly knew her at all, and from every indication the young lieutenant could barely stand to be in the same room as he, forever fidgeting or sputtering uncomfortably like she'd done in the meeting chamber earlier.

Nevin draped the damp towel about his hips, feeling the tired muscles in his body ache from the harsh workout he'd subjected himself to. The thing was, Anna didn't know him, he thought, examining his nearly naked body in the mirror, the battlefield of scars across his dusky skin. She knew nothing of the man he was in private. They needed a chance to get to know one another; time alone where they might let down their respective guards.

With a sudden burst of resolve, he glanced at his

communicator, and arrived at a plan—a perfect plan, in fact, if only he could enact it without raising Anna's suspicions.

Chapter One

Four months later

"It's just a short sortie over to the mitres, in and out of the location to examine the chamber's exterior." Anika described the mission, reading instructions from her handheld.

Of all the assignments. Anna shook her head in disbelief, nodding toward the far side of the hangar where Nevin Daniels went through pre-flight check. "With him?" she complained. "Anika, you know what he—"

But her twin cut her off with a raised hand. "Commander Bennett requested you to accompany Lieutenant Daniels. Specifically."

Anna's face burned. "What am I supposed to talk to the guy about, huh? It's the fourth mission in as many months—and he never says a word to me."

"He's serious, that's all."

"He intimidates me—I admit it."

Her twin sister's nose scrunched up, a strange smile lighting her face. "I didn't think anyone could ever intimidate you. At least not for long."

"I'm telling you, Nevin Daniels does not *talk* to me. Nada. Stuck in the aircraft, pitch black dark, he won't say a thing." Anna threw both hands in the air, frustrated and...feeling something she didn't care to examine too closely. "Oh, *Medshki!*"

Her sister placed a firm hand on her shoulder. "Can't you just tune out and think about something else?"

Anna made an exasperated cry. "Not when I'm that close to him. Gods, no."

Her sister gave a sly, knowing smile. "Uh-huh."

"It will be my own personal hell, that's what I'm saying."

"Really? And here I was thinking you'd be shrieking with joy just to have another assignment with the fine lieutenant."

"Oh, please shut up." Anna ducked out of her twin's grasp. "Ever since Riley moved onto base, you've been insufferable."

"Because I want my sister happy? To know what it's like to have a bondmate?"

Anna cringed. "You do realize you're talking about one of our most superior officers, right?"

Her sister's warm eyes lit with mischief. "The same officer you've been interested in for months?"

Make that years, she wanted to add, but only shook her head. "Based on what? A glance across a meeting table?"

Anika gazed across the hangar, watching as Nevin

looked over a flight check list. "Doesn't it seem odd to you that he'd be requesting you, over and over," her sister asked, "on these routine assignments?"

"Wait a minute." Anna poked at the air between them significantly. "You said the commander was pairing me up with Daniels."

Anika shrugged. "I'm not sure how it's coming down exactly; I just know it keeps happening and it didn't used to before that meeting room"—Anika formed quotation marks in the air with her fingers—"incident."

Anna sighed, glancing across the hangar deck to where the devil himself stood inspecting the small, stealth aircraft that would carry them to the mitres location some time after nightfall. "He's too serious, never laughs," she complained. "Plus, he's not even nice."

Anika's gaze tracked across the hangar once again, lingering on the lieutenant, and she laughed. "He certainly *looks* nice."

"From this far away, sure." Anna snorted.

"Well, you'd know—you've been looking at him from this distance for long enough."

Anna glared at her twin, who only grinned back at her, and had the distinct impression that it wasn't the commander who'd even issued this particular assignment—but her own damned sister.

The helmet would leave her hair mashed and her face

imprinted. Ridiculous, but that was pretty much the level of Anna's thoughts as Nevin launched them out of the hangar and into the inky mountainside nighttime. They would be completely undetectable in this small, sleek craft—their test pilots had taken these Phoenix models all around the earth in order to test their stealth capabilities. None of the planes had ever popped up on the humans' radar.

At least she knew she was in good hands, she thought wryly, listening to the heavy sound of her own breathing inside the oxygen mask. *What if he thinks I'm breathing heavier than normal? What if he knows that he's got my heart beating like crazy?*

She watched over Nevin's shoulder as he worked the controls. Damn, even his hands turned her on, what with the black gloves fitting like a second skin, making him seem all fighter pilot. She couldn't help it—pilots in general had always, always turned her on—and Nevin's taking her on these sorties had done absolutely nothing to dampen her enthusiasm for *him* in particular.

He startled her when he cut right over the mountains, and with his left hand, rapped on the canopy. With a gesture, he indicated the view below, and she pressed up against the dark glass to discover the twinkling lights of town.

"Very pretty," she breathed through the comm.

"It's always beautiful to me." His husky voice, so immediate and right in her ears, was like the feel of velvet across her skin. She shivered, and he continued,

"Everything here is still so pure, so...pristine. Especially the snow."

By the gods, the lieutenant was actually conversing with her—and opening up to her. It was the first time in all these months, the first little breakthrough since their "moment" in the meeting room.

"Do you miss it?" She leaned forward in her seat, just slightly, yearning to be closer to him.

"Miss our home?" He shook his head. "Not very much, I'm afraid. It's easy to grow accustomed to our more peaceful existence here."

Peaceful? They spent all their time on the run from Antousians and humans, while trying to just protect humanity from the same fate that had befallen their own planet.

"I'm surprised you would call things on Earth peaceful."

"I haven't been shot in the six years I've spent here." His husky, throaty laugh rang in both her ears.

"You were shot back on Refaria?" she asked incredulously. This was something she'd never once heard about the man.

"Three times," he told her in a formal, clipped tone.

After a long moment of waiting for him to elaborate, she pressed, "When? Which battles?"

He made a sudden adjustment with the throttle, and her unanswered question hung suspended between them for what felt a near-eternity. "Sir?" She reached forward and touched his shoulder, wondering if perhaps he'd not heard her question. "Which battles?"

She kept her gaze trained on the back of his helmet, watched as he turned to glance at her hand briefly. Still, he said nothing.

Blowing out a heavy sigh, she stared at the black sky above the plane's canopy. Probably way too loud—so loud, in fact, that the lieutenant could read her frustration with him.

"Lieutenant Draekus," he told her gently, "as my fellow soldier, surely you understand the ghosts that still haunt me...ghosts from our home."

Unbidden, tears prickled Anna's eyes. Tears of comprehension and sympathy; tears of the connection that they shared in their lost home world. Nothing on Refaria would ever be the same again, and she understood that it wasn't the battles so much; it was the heartbreak of what had befallen them all that kept Nevin Daniels from talking.

"Of course, sir," she whispered into the comm link, and gave his shoulder a slight pat before removing her hand.

He brought the craft in low over the lake, and it was a perfect, routine approach until the last moment when a loud scraping sound began beneath the underbelly of the plane. There was a jolting jerk that sent Anna's head slamming into the side of the canopy. For what seemed a long time, everything went black until she heard herself muttering a string of expletives in low Refarian. Her head felt as if a grenade had exploded inside her helmet, and strange lights were flashing in front of her eyes. She clasped at her helmet, wishing she could rub the side of her skull.

"What's going on?" she slurred, feeling the craft tilt and gyrate. Dimly, she realized the terrain below looked all wrong, that they weren't anywhere near their planned landing area.

"Hang on, Anna!" Nevin worked frantically with the controls, flipping switches and struggling to control the craft. A bright red warning light flashed within the cockpit, then a woman's urgent voice began, listing off a series of malfunctions. Funny, but even though she should have been upset, Anna felt oddly calm, noticing that the emergency warnings were programmed in English, not Refarian. *Maybe in case the plane is ever captured by human officials.*

Capture, she thought dully, the world growing dim again. *Sure hope we don't get our asses captured after we crash...*

Nevin circled the downed craft, trying to assess what, precisely, had gone wrong. Trailing his fingertips along the plane's side, he emitted his natural energy, working to power the machine. No reaction. With a quick glance back at where Anna lay off to the side, unconscious—he'd carried her there immediately in case the craft blew—he opened both of his palms.

Dropping to the ground so he wouldn't have to steady himself, he concentrated on his open hands. He cupped them in front of his chest, closed his eyes, and allowed his natural energy to build. It was his one true blessing from All, his gift of energy; that it was such a markedly unusual one only made it all the more special. Perhaps now it would be the thing that could save both their lives; if his natural power could somehow infuse the craft—if it had been a simple matter of a ruptured tank—then he might be able to power them back out of this isolated place.

A glowing ball of pure energy formed between his hands, and manipulating it carefully, he began directing it toward the plane.

Behind him, Anna's soft voice startled him. "I've never seen anything quite like that before."

He focused his entire being on wielding the power sphere, but nevertheless, it changed hues from a bright golden shade to a warmer and richer one. Of course his energy would react to Anna; if there were any woman alive on this planet who could cause a reaction like that, it would be her.

"I have to...use it. Wait."

"It's your energy, isn't it?"

"Anna...a moment," he barely managed to gasp before finally catapulting the powerful orb of energy into the craft. He watched as it seemed to explode into a million pinpricks of glowing power, then hoisted himself back into the cockpit and, in vain, attempted to start the damned thing once again. After several long moments of manipulating the controls, he dropped back to the ground, and strode purposefully to Anna's side.

"How are you feeling?" He took her bare hand into his own gloved one. "You took quite a nasty hit to the head."

She smiled up at him wanly. "Not so good."

Searching the area around them, he knew he had to get her someplace safe for the night. Bears were already coming out of hibernation, and there were wolves and other predators. "We could sleep in the plane," he suggested. "Probably the safest bet tonight."

Her eyes drifted shut. "I wanna lie down."

"You don't really need that, Anna. In fact, you should stay awake until we can determine the extent of your injuries."

"Can we at least warm up? Make a fire or something first?" She struggled to sit up. "Wait! I have an idea. I just need to shapeshift, then I can go for help."

Anna pressed a hand to her temple. "I know I can," she insisted, but by the way her face drained of color, she was obviously fighting a wave of nausea, "Just a minute..." she attempted weakly.

Nevin cupped her shoulder, aware that the warmth of his body radiated through his glove and her uniform, but he didn't move his hand. He liked the idea of her feeling his heat, and besides, he had the perfect excuse: She needed his warm touch after tonight's shock.

"You need to rest, Anna. It would be dangerous for

you to shapeshift and make that long trek back to base. You might grow too weak."

"I'd be fine," she tried to argue, but he cut her off.

"Lieutenant, I am ordering you to stay here, with the downed craft, and pass the nighttime hours within the cockpit." His voice was stern and pointed. "Understood?"

From where she lay staring up at him, she gave him a weak salute. This earned her a grudging, sideways smile from her commanding officer. "Good work, soldier," he said, returning her salute.

Looking back over his shoulder at the craft, he thought through the logistics of the cramped space. He had to determine the best way to help Anna recuperate without putting her through any more pain—and without winding up holding her in his arms which was, truthfully, the thing he wanted most desperately of all. More, even, than getting the craft working again. It was pure insanity, but once he'd landed safely his first thoughts had been of Anna. Of having her all to himself, here in the wilds, of them being alone for some period of time. It had taken everything within him to assume command of the situation as his training dictated.

"You never answered about your energy," she called out to him softly. He spun to face her, shocked by the vulnerable expression on her face. "I've never seen anything so beautiful in my life."

Nevin's entire body tensed, grew tighter than a drum. "It's nothing."

"You should have told me that day in the meeting

room. If I'd known that you had the gift of energy, I'd have trusted you with my Madjin mark. I'd have shown you."

He wasn't sure how it happened, but suddenly he had both hands braced about her face, leaning over her. His breathing was intense, his hunger for her so palpable and real, he could feel it coursing throughout his body. Damn it, she was injured, but he couldn't stop himself. He drew his mouth close to hers and whispered, "One's energy, Anna, is quite personal. Remember? You said it."

His whole body blazed with unleashed heat; his chest rose and fell with heavy pants, but still he stayed hovering just over her. "Intimate, Anna," he continued, feeling his cock harden at the thought of her having seen his own energy—and of her showing him her mark.

She stared up into his eyes, her gaze flitting over his features, down to his chest, back up to his eyes again. "Yes, that's all true." He'd never heard her voice so hoarse, so rich and filled with emotion. "But you let me see yours."

He shook his head, adamant. "Inadvertently."

She reached a hand to his face, tracing the outline of his jaw. "Show me again, Lieutenant."

He lifted off of her, ruing his actions. Maybe he was the one who'd hit his head. He gave it a light shake, adjusting his pants as he turned from her, afraid that she'd see the prominent hard-on that she'd just given him. "We need to get back inside the plane for the night."

"Show me again," she repeated, and suddenly she was behind him—right behind him—and he froze. Both of his hands were against the wing and both of hers were flat against the middle of his back. "What are you doing, Anna Draekus?" She kept her hands there, right against his body, the only thing separating his skin from hers the thin material of his uniform.

"I'm not sure." She snorted with laughter. "I hit my head and woooo! Suddenly I go all *sla'skai* on you." Her hands dropped away; he heard her take several steps back, but still he could only stand, both hands gripping the wing as if it were a lifeline. If only he'd turned; if only he'd been able to transcend his natural shyness and had kissed her like he yearned to do.

But the moment was gone.

Chapter Two

Nowhere to stretch, nowhere to get comfortable, and sleep just wasn't happening in the rear of Nevin's cockpit. *What a word,* she thought in amusement. *Here I am, alone in the man's cockpit, my feet practically in his lap, and we're both trying to sleep.*

Nevin on the other hand, seemed to be dozing nicely. She sighed, rubbed at her head, and shifted her right foot until it was propped on his right thigh. He stirred in the seat in front of her, nestling his head against the back of his seat, and slid a warm, gloved palm over her foot. Her entire body lit with fire—deep, mystic fire, the kind only a Refarian warrior like Nevin could possibly set within her.

Wake up, she thought, wiggling her toes. "Nevin," she murmured, burning warmth radiating from where his hand covered her foot.

"Hmm?" he asked sleepily, and only then did she realize she'd whispered his name aloud.

"Uh, nothing."

She felt him tense, his fingers twitched against her instep, and she knew he was going to move away—or move her foot, even worse. She stretched her toes, flexing them, and slid her foot a little closer toward the interior of his thigh. Although she only had a view of the back of his head, she could tell that he stared down into his lap, uncertain—until, at last, he slid his fingers back around her instep, gently massaging the bottom of her foot.

She leaned back in the seat, staring at the twinkling lights above their closed canopy. "Will they be able to track us?" she voiced into the darkness between them.

"Probably. Depends on the state of the craft, any number of factors." He kept his voice low, hushed, and the sound of it in such an intimate space caused her body to tighten in sharp awareness of him.

He kept rubbing her foot, working his thumb and fingers along her instep. Without meaning to she released a soft moan. "That's...amazing."

"Give me the other one." His voice was husky, throaty with need—a need that she had no trouble guessing at because she felt it just like he did. "I'll rub both."

She swallowed, carefully sliding her left foot onto his other thigh, keenly aware that she practically had her legs wrapped about his waist—well, if only he weren't in the seat in front of her. Still, the suggestive position, the proximity of her feet to his most intimate areas, caused the place between her legs to grow warm and damp.

In the darkness, she heard his breathing quicken as he took hold of her other foot, rubbing it as he'd done the first. She closed her eyes, and slowly—ever so slowly—inched her right foot inward between his thighs. It didn't take long for her to bump into a hard ridge, long and thick against his thigh. When she curled her toes against it, Nevin physically jolted in the seat with a low-pitched groan of pure pleasure.

He said nothing; she didn't utter a thing, but for many silent moments she massaged his erection, then worked her toes between his thighs, back and forth across his balls until he slammed a fist against the side of the canopy, uttering her name over and over. "Gods, help me!" he cried out, turning in the seat.

When their eyes locked for that first moment, she could hardly breathe. She'd never seen so much passion and need in any one man's gaze. "You have to stop, Anna," he hissed in a tight voice, staring at her over his seat back. "Now. Gods, as it is…" He shook his head, muttering a quiet curse in Refarian.

"I can finish what I started," she offered with a defiant smile.

Again, he slammed a fist against the canopy, putting his back to her. With a gentle shove, he moved her feet out of his lap. "We need rest—*you* need rest, Anna, to recover from your injuries."

"You didn't like that?" The question was sincere; she wasn't a virgin, but she didn't have a long list of men in her past either. "Was it not pleasurable?"

Nevin made a tight sound as if he were gritting his teeth. "It was the most pleasure I've felt in such a long time, Anna."

She leaned forward, wrapping her arms about his neck and pressing her mouth close to his left ear. "Then why stop?"

He touched her arm lightly. "Because I'm your commanding officer—and I have to lead you in this army. Because"—he blew out an edgy breath—"I'm too old for you, and, Anna, because with as much as I crave you, I don't trust myself to be honorable. Not out here, not in the wilds."

"Who said anything about being honorable?" she countered, releasing a hot breath against his cheek.

He jerked his head sideways. "This isn't going to happen between us, Lieutenant." He sounded every bit the pompous, tight-assed leader she'd always thought him to be. "I will not allow it to."

"Fine, sir. Just perfectly fine." She sank back into her seat, feeling humiliated and confused. "But just one thing: If you didn't want this, then why have you worked so hard to make it happen? All these sorties, everything?"

She studied his profile as he gazed sideways, staring out the canopy. His expression was thoughtful, and far more emotion-filled than she would have imagined—and all of her anger faded away. Nevin Daniels was a man constantly at war with himself; she'd only just begun to figure that out.

He pressed a gloved hand against his temple, giving his head a light shake. "You have always left me muddled and confused, Anna Draekus. If my behavior regarding you is inconsistent, I have only that to blame."

Always? Always muddled and confused? That one simple word would imply that he'd *always* been aware of her, thinking of her, which changed absolutely everything between them. Including the new determination it forced within her, the need to penetrate the reserved lieutenant's superficial coolness—to get to the heart of the lion hidden within—and unleash him.

Chapter Three

Nevin squatted down beside the bubbling stream, propping an arm against his knee as he watched the cold, rushing water. "We have to find a way to store some of this in our pack."

"We can fill the plastic bag from mine." It had been almost a full day without any sign or hope of rescue. Anna had worked to shapeshift earlier in the afternoon, but the magnetic energy emitted from all the volcanic activity in the area—as well as from the mitres—had made it impossible for her to do so. Just as, they figured, it made it equally impossible for the base to track their downed craft. Finally, in the mid-afternoon they'd set off on a quest for fresh water, and had just located a good source after only two hours of hiking and searching. They exchanged a grateful look; each knew only too well that they might have come up empty-handed for much longer.

Nevin gave a brisk nod. "Good." Totally serious, ever the commanding officer—but then his dark face broke into a mischievous smile. "But first I'm getting some now." He shoved both shirt sleeves up, revealing dark, muscular forearms dusted with black silky hairs. The clinging synthetic material of his uniform shirt tugged across his powerful shoulders, revealing every indentation, every ripple of his defined musculature.

Anna trailed her tongue across her lips, watching as he bent low over the stream, cupping one hand and drawing water up toward his wide, full mouth. His slanted, almond-shaped eyes narrowed in pleasure as he skimmed water to his lips, over and over, until rivulets ran down his chin, gleaming on his dusky growth of beard.

But then something arrested him, and he froze mid-gesture, sliding his gaze upward until he stared at her on the opposite bank where she stood ogling him shamelessly. The corners of his damp mouth quirked upward, and she knew he'd read the desire in her eyes.

"It tastes delicious." His tone was suggestive; he wiped his mouth with the back of his hand—never taking his black gaze off of her. He'd busted her totally, discovered her gazing at him with absolute lust.

"I'm sure it is." She bent over, leaning from atop the bank and reached low with her hand for some of the flowing water. It was a long reach and all at once, she slipped, almost falling face-first into the stream. Catching hold of a clump of tall grass, she steadied herself.

"Need some help? I can come across, if need be."

She heard the wolf in his tone. "I've got it all right." *Oh I just bet you'd love to help me.* But she had a plan now—a pretty simple and direct one—to make him work harder. To let him take the lead; somehow, that seemed to be the key to getting him to open up to her.

"Well"—he laughed, a deep and rumbling sound—"let me know if I can be of any service. Perhaps hold you from behind while you bend down so you don't fall in face-first."

"Nope, got it." She dug her heels into the ground behind her, her face flushing, and with a quickly tossed glare at Nevin, took another few sips.

When she had drunk her fill, the two of them took up positions on opposite sides of the stream bed, eyeing each other. He'd unsnapped his uniform top, damp with sweat and creek water, and it fell open to the middle of his sternum, revealing a tightly sculpted chest that seemed nearly impossible to contain within the stretchy fabric.

She reached for a stone and tossed it into the rushing water, avoiding his steady, piercing gaze. What did he want from her? What did he expect? That she'd jump down from her position, traipse through the water, and throw herself at him brazenly?

He'd always seemed so stern. Totally buttoned up. Too intense and humorless. But the man she'd been discovering here in the woods as they wandered and wandered trying to find their way out alive was virile and dangerous. Barely restricted in his desires, much more like the sensuous man she'd encountered during her interrogation.

His gaze was still fixed on her, totally unwavering and she noticed that the late day sun caught the silver in his hair, making it practically glow against his rich, golden-red skin. The man had the pure look of the ancient Refarians, with his very high cheekbones and slanted eyes, the arching dark brows. All of that, when coupled with the dramatic silver in his hair, gave him the exotic look of a primeval warrior, of a tribal leader who might come roaring out of the mountains.

She thought about the rumors she'd always heard about mature men like Nevin. It was said they became full-on rutting stallions in bed after their change. Her mind supplied a slip-silver image of Nevin, gloriously nude, rising beneath the full moon like a *rpt'ai* beast, ready to devour and take her by the sheer weight and power of his dominance. She shivered despite the warm sun, watching him across the stream; he appraised her likewise, his black eyes narrowing hungrily.

Oh, yes, he definitely had the classic look of the ancient Refarians. Some murmured that he had royal blood in his lineage since the D'Aravni and D'Ashani males all matured at a younger age than other non-royals. She could easily recall the day about a year ago when he'd strutted into the kitchen, as smug as she always thought he seemed, and with blazing eyes had defied a damn soul to comment on the change in his hair color. It had taken all of three days for his thick, gleaming black hair to turn.

No one had murmured a word. No one even so much as thought about gossiping or snickering behind Lieutenant Daniels' back. He was that sort of leader—so serious, so incorruptible, and always just a little bit dour.

Until these past hours when all of a sudden it was as if the ground beneath them had cracked open, as if the universe had tilted askew and she'd seen the lieutenant for the sensuous creature he truly was—had obviously always been, but kept it hidden behind a carefully constructed veneer of leadership.

She focused on the rocks along the shore, tossing them into the water one by one.

"You shan't do that forever, I hope?" he called to her, ever his formal self.

"Yeah? What else you got in mind, sir?"

At first she thought he wasn't going to answer, but then a wicked grin filled his face and he rose to his feet, beckoning her toward him with the crook of his index finger. "Come over here, Anna."

"Oh—I better not." She laughed nervously, sliding backward on her bottom.

He took another step closer, to the very edge of the embankment. "Anna," he told her intensely, leveling her with his midnight gaze, "I said to come over here to me."

She shook her head, a soft sigh blowing across her lips. "Why?"

"I need you to understand something."

Slowly she stepped to her feet, and surveyed the flowing water below. It was shallow, but she'd get her boots wet.

"Wait!" he called, and swung his legs over the edge, dropping down onto the damp rocks. With a bold leap, he crossed the water, stopping just beneath where she stood. "I forgot my manners for a moment. Forgive me."

He had to squint as he gazed upward because of the late day sun, and he lifted a hand to shield his eyes. With his other he reached for her. "Jump down to me," he urged huskily. "I'll catch you so you won't get wet."

She slid, more than jumped, into his arms, and found herself braced between a pair of powerful, bulging biceps—pinned against an even firmer and more powerful chest. Frozen for several bottomless seconds, she could only stare into his thick-lashed eyes, aware of the intense beating of his heart, of the feel of heat radiating off of his body.

Then with a slight laugh, an almost self-conscious one, he swung her down beside him onto the rocks where he stood.

She smoothed her uniform out—as if anything could help it after the hiking and desperate climbing—and then looked up into his eyes. "You wanted to show me something?"

Without a word he bent his head, lowering it until his face was pressed right up against hers, until they were cheek to cheek. She felt the rough sandpaper of his unshaven face, smelled the woods on him and she stiffened. Waiting. What the hell was he going to do? He moved his lips right up to the tickling spot behind her ear and sucked in a long, staggered breath; then blew it out, whooshing right into her ear. He was scenting her! The bastard hadn't asked—he'd tricked her.

She lifted both hands, ready to shove him away from her. But he reached out and pulled her palms tenderly against his chest. "Wait, Anna. Give me a moment. Please."

It was all in the way he said please. As if everything in his world depended upon her granting the request, as if he couldn't live or take another breath if she wouldn't just let him stay close to her for another moment. She could have melted into the earth right on the spot.

"Oh-okay," she whispered, and once again he drew in a long, hungry breath, pushing his mouth right up to the side of her face, moving it upward along her hairline, then back down to her cheek, nuzzling. He gasped when he finished, making a tight, barely controlled noise in the back of his throat.

"Now me," he urged in a voice she hardly recognized. Its timbre was that of pure, unmitigated lust. "Scent me, Anna." Then he added, almost with a touching innocence, "It's all right."

Reaching upward, she clutched both of his shoulders and with a nod of understanding, she pressed her face against his chest and gave a light, tentative sniff—just the shortest little burst to test his scent. It was the very first of the Refarian mating rituals, that need to drink in your potential lover's aroma. To see if it aroused you.

That one light burst and he totally infused her, sent fire into the deepest part of her being; burrowing closer, she took a longer, deeper drink of the man's aroma—and her entire being exploded into thousands of particles of desire. A wave of such keen need and longing swept over her that her knees almost buckled. Sliding a hand behind the small of her back, Nevin steadied her.

Oh gods, it was the pheromones. He was covered up in them, so heady it was all she could do not to jump him without another word. It had to be the hormones from his recent maturity change.

"Y-you should have warned me," she hardly managed, pressing her face into the folds of his uniform shirt—but instead her lips met warm, soft skin where his shirt had fallen open.

One large hand skimmed along her back. "Warned you about what? That our scents would be such an explosive"—she heard him swallow—"maddening mix?"

"About your gods-forsaken pheromones!" She bunched his uniform in both fists, yearning for another inhalation of his scent. Frustrated to an almost painful level. "Your hormones are at a fever pitch...you should have said something." She twisted his shirt in both hands, a plaintive cry of frustration escaping her lips.

He pulled back, staring down into her eyes and gave a light shake of his head. "I don't know what you mean."

"I *felt* what happened! When I scented you! I may be inexperienced, but I'm not stupid—I know about men in their maturity, how compulsively sexual you are."

One corner of Nevin's full mouth turned upward in gentle amusement. "Anna, I hate to break this to you— but I'm not emitting any pheromones. What you felt?" he cupped her cheek meaningfully, tilting her face upward until her gaze locked with his. "That was just me."

She shook her head, intending to back away, but

instead tightened one hand about his upper arm. "That's not possible."

Wrapping both arms about her, he fixed her against his chest. "What have you heard, exactly, about men in their maturity?" He wasn't mocking her; the question was gentle. Genuine. At utter odds with his purely masculine body, his intense and arousing scent that had almost leveled her to the very ground beneath them.

"That you rut like fucking stallions," she blurted, then, wincing in embarrassment added, "Is that true?"

"I wouldn't know," he whispered against the top of her head. "I've not been given the opportunity to find out."

She shoved at his chest, stepping backward. "Oh, just stop it, Nevin." It seemed ridiculous to call him "sir" or bother with their military formalities. "You must think me a stupid little fool."

He cocked his head sideways, watching her. "Do I strike you as a man with much time for relationships? For any sort of emotional entanglements whatsoever, Anna? Truly?"

She blew out a breath, staring at the ground between them and wishing that her face weren't blazing so hot.

"Anna?"

Slowly she shook her head. "I've never known you to have any women in your life."

"I won't lie to you," he said softly. "I think you'd know that about me by now."

"Do you think the speculations are true?" She barely

dared to look up at him. "About men of your...well, um, your age?"

He scowled. "How old, precisely, do you think that I am?"

"Thirty-eight," she volunteered easily. "You told me that day in the meeting room."

"You remember that day?" His voice deepened, filled with emotion.

She closed her eyes, hands trembling slightly at the memory. "Of course."

"Yes, thirty-eight, and perhaps truly too old for you. In my maturity now, as you can plainly see." He raked his fingers through the silver spiking hairs atop his head in order to drive the point home. "You are still so young, full of energy and time, whereas I"—his voice broke off and he seemed to struggle with something—"I have lived too many lives already. So you're absolutely correct to be wary, Anna. Back away from me."

Perhaps it was his awkward denials and attempts at reversing their moment, but she felt suddenly very certain about what he meant to her. What he would mean, what he had already come to mean over the past day and months.

She placed a palm over his heart, felt its urgent, steady beating. "You aren't an old man, Nevin. Look at you! You're so handsome!" With her fingertips, she reached upward and traced the slight lines about his eyes. "You wear your maturity like the virile man that you are. I know what maturity is about, don't think that I don't." She laughed, reaching her hand to the top of his head, stroking it, feeling the scratch of the close-cropped hairs, running them under her hands like *zia* grass back home, all prickly and tickling. "You are in your sexual prime, it's obvious." He stiffened beneath her touch, shaking his head slightly.

"Not...true." He drew in a shuddering breath.

"No?" she teased, pulling back slightly to study him. "Then why are you trembling so badly when I touch you? Because you're dead inside? Because you have no life left? And why did you insist that we scent each other?" He said nothing, kept his face unreadable. "Because you know," she finished, leaning up onto her tiptoes so she could meet his gaze head-on. "Because you understand this thing between us."

He released a rumbling, low growl from the back of his throat, like a Refarian tiger in heat. She had friends who had lovers like Nevin, sexy, unstoppable men in their post-change prime; everyone said such men were volcanoes in bed, unable to suppress their ever-increasing needs.

Nevin fit those descriptions to perfection, both physically and emotionally. Mentally. His stamina was undeniable—they'd hiked these mountains for hours and he'd never tired. She loved that in a man, someone who could keep pace with her boundless energy. She knew what he'd be in bed: that same tiger in heat.

"I-I am not the man for you, Anna," he stammered, lifting his chin proudly. But he could do nothing to dampen his distinctive, sexual scent. It was palpable, strong as she breathed him in and his aroma kept tantalizing her. Why All had put the Refarian men in their prime of heat *after* their fertility faded, well this much she'd never understood. Was there some mystical secret to it? She had no idea for certain, but the man before her shook with barely contained lust—lust so profound it gave off a scent that kept her entire body tethered to his like a chain of reflexive Antousian metal.

"I can still scent you," she told him at last, running her tongue over her lips. "It's intense, Nevin. The aroma of heat and fertility and gods-only-knows what all."

With a tremor, he lifted his hand to her throat, stroking the slight indentation at the base of it, running his fingertips across her bare skin. "Anna...back away. I was wrong to invite this. You're much too young, too innocent. Nothing right can happen here."

"*You're* not backing away." She gave a defiant lift of her chin. "You're touching me."

"One of us must...break this hold we seem to have"— he hesitated, his breathing growing heavy as he wrestled for words—"upon each other. This lusty hold. Must stop, Anna. Must."

"Then do it. Do it, Nevin. You make the break."

He dipped his fingers lower, tracing the edge of her collar. "I don't think I'm capable."

"Then make love to me—here, now, beneath the sun and sky!" She lifted both arms upward in proclamation. "Take me, *N'vsai!*" she cried, invoking his Refarian name.

"Take my body beneath yours and prove to me just how alive you really are."

His black eyebrows drew together in a querulous V-shape. With his mouth he blew out agitated, hot breaths against her face. "You have no idea what you ask, Anna."

"I have every idea," she fired back coquettishly, wrapping both arms about his neck. She draped herself upon him, working her hips up against his, forming around his body. "Whatever you want, Nevin, I'll give it to you. Just relax. Feel it. Don't hold back so much."

Chapter Four

He was at a perilous moment of indecision. This woman, this Madjin, had tested his will and his discipline; she'd unmasked every fear in his heart about his manhood and virility. She'd awakened slumbering memories of what it was to love a woman, to feel young and randy and high on sex play. "You say you know about men like me. Mature men, men filled with this-this"—he held out his hands by explanation—"this kind of want."

"So you're thirty-eight. So you need sex—a lot of sex. Guess what, Nevin? I need it too." Anna's wide smile spread across her face. He'd never seen a more radiant, beautiful smile on any person, so filled as it often was with unmitigated joy and happiness at some discovery or another. In this case, the discovery being...him. "And I need you, Nevin—not later, but now."

His entire body grew taut and ready; at the slightest touch from her, there would be no more constraining himself. With a voice that quavered, he held out his last excuse, the only real reason he held back at all: Their significant age gap. "When I was serving Jared's father, you were still toddling." Quickly, he did the math. Yes, he'd come under the king's guidance at the tender age of seventeen. She would have been just seven years old.

"Hardly!" She snorted gracelessly, sliding against him, running both hands up and down his back. "I was almost eight. I remember seeing you—did you know that?"

He gaped back at her, unable to fathom that she told the truth. "What?"

She nodded. "I was at the palace still, with the other Madjin," she explained. "It was just before Jared's parents were murdered."

"Yes, that was when I came to serve the king." Nevin thought back to those early years. "A few months before."

"I'd been a naughty shapeshifter," she told him throatily. "I pretended to be a grown woman—got in much trouble for that, by the way. I talked to you in the hallway. I thought you were...so handsome. Totally mysterious." She actually released a dreamy little sigh at the supposed memory.

"You are lying now, Anna," he cried. "You must be."

"No, it's true. It's always been true."

"You were only a little girl—"

"I gave you directions—that very first day."

Nevin wracked his brain, trying to remember what the woman was talking about. Directions? Had she always remembered this, been waiting until right now to rip open his world? Gods, what if he'd come on to her? She'd only been a child! What was she telling him?

In a panic, he shoved her apart from him, turning

brusquely away. "Enough with the games, Anna! Enough. You can't have me simply because you've decided you must."

"I've heard that a lot in my time, but I've pretty much discovered that if I'm determined enough, I can have whatever—and whomever—I want. And I want you, Nevin. You have no idea what you do to me."

He spun upon her. "Tell me what you're talking about, from all those years ago."

She sighed, smiling faintly. For many long moments she didn't speak, but then at last she slowly raised her eyes to meet his. When she did, he knew that this was no joke or teasing on her part: Anna had always remembered that day.

"You came at night," she began softly, "in your transport. It was compact...and fast. All the Madjin whispered about it, buzzing that you had the latest model. I agreed to sneak out with them. Marco took the lead. He was older than me, about a year, and I liked to follow him around. He had a good sense of adventure, about the interesting things. So I went with him. We went around the side yard, through the garden." Her voice grew more reflective and she looked up at the darkening sky. "The night was so clear, I could have read a book in that garden. I took Marco's hand when he extended it behind him, and then...there you were. Standing by your black, shiny transport, instructing the security patrol as to the proper way to dock it. You had such a beautiful face; I'd never seen anyone quite so handsome before. The way your eyes were slightly slanted—just like now," she said, gesturing toward his face, "your long black hair, tied at your nape with a silver chord. You seemed the most exotic man I'd ever seen."

"I did wear my hair just that way," he agreed. "And I had that new model transport."

"You came from money, that's what they all whispered." Guiltily, he nodded it to be the truth. In the old time, he'd had more money than any young man should have ever been given, and had always enjoyed spending it beyond measure. That had been before.

"So, when the others snuck back to our compound, I stayed behind. They never realized they'd lost me. I shapeshifted and made myself a lady of the court. You paused and stared at me for at least ten seconds, I think, before asking me directions to the king's assembly hall."

"I have no memory of that." But he did. Gods help him, he surely did. The lady had seemed to personify the life he would live at the palace. He'd been star-struck, as taken with her beauty as he was with the other finery at the court. In every possible way, he'd been a fool. Valued all the wrong things. Never realized how fragile and tentative life was—that it was a gift.

"It doesn't matter," she told him frankly. "I just wanted you to know that even then, so many years ago, I thought you as beautiful as I do now. Only you've grown more seasoned and handsome."

"And older," he whispered, reminding her again of the chasm that separated them—she with her breathy youth, he his settled maturity.

She shrugged. "Thirty-eight isn't old, not to the humans and certainly not to our species. You know that. It's just a flimsy argument because I frighten you," she told him self-confidently.

"How did you gain all this control?" he hissed. "When did it happen? At what point did it cease being about your mistakes and about my lust? Please, school me, Anna, for I missed the moment."

She laughed in his face, reaching a sure hand to cup his cheek. "Do you feel controlled, Lieutenant?"

"Completely," he confessed as she sidled up against him once again. With perfect accuracy she molded her much more compact body against his imposing one. She cupped his hips, taking hold of him. All at once he found himself falling into a thrusting motion with her, mimicking the act itself. He went harder inside his pants, his cock infused with blood and need before he could take a breath. The woman had him on a leash. It would not do. It would not do at all.

Like a bull let loose, he charged her. Swung her up onto the bank and plowed her to the ground, tumbling her body beneath his, unable to quash his pulsating need for another moment. She squirmed beneath him, trying to catch her breath, but he'd give her no quarter. "You were warned, Anna," he thundered against her cheek, pushing her body fully beneath his. "I told you to back away."

"Yes, Nevin—you did." She trembled as he sniffed at her face, her neck, her hands. Drawing her scent hard into his own tight body.

"You don't know where you've brought us," he warned. "No idea what this life change in me has done."

"Yes, I do...I feel it."

He let loose a sputtering of curses, frisking her body, searching for the opening to her pants. He fumbled, missed his mark, then thrust his hands down into her panties, never bothering with the fastenings. With a growling cry, he tossed back his head, making his mating urges known to the forest around them. In the distance he swore he heard a wolf cry in return. He *felt* wolfish, wild and needy.

They rolled together on the earth—first he on top, then she, then he again, tumbling and laughing and lusting together. His shirt vanished, her pants crumpled into a heap; one item of clothing after another was discarded until he found himself kneeling before her, gloriously naked.

"Your body," she whispered breathlessly, gesturing with her hand. "Look at you. I've never seen anything quite like you."

Self-consciously he stared down at his chest, wondering what she saw. For a moment, he glimpsed himself through her eyes. He was chiseled, completely so. He always had been and in recent months he'd been training harder than ever in a desperate effort to expend just this very energy. It had profited nothing. He was filled to the hilt with sensual stirrings such as he'd never known, not even in his youth.

"Look at *you*," he countered softly, studying the way

Anna's porcelain skin glowed beneath the late day sun. It was as if the sun itself had touched her, she was glorious, curving and full-bodied in a way that caused his erection to leap as he stared at her.

They each studied the other, kneeling face to face, palm to palm. A sudden stillness fell over them, slowing things, all his crazy need for rutting falling away. There was only Anna...beautiful, graceful, spirited Anna, right before him.

She seemed every bit as taken with him as he was with her. "I have no words," he offered softly. "Only my touch."

"Then give me that." She arched her back so that her silky black hair fell across her shoulders.

With his fingertips he drew a line from her collarbone down to her right breast, trailing his fingers hotly across her smooth skin. When he reached her nipple, he circled it with his forefinger in a rough motion, causing it to bead beneath his touch. It had been years since he'd held a woman like this; it had been months since he'd been able to stop thinking of Anna.

Staring at her lithe body, naked and perfect, he battled himself for one final moment. Deep inside he couldn't shake the sense that he was all wrong for her; he was past the age of giving her children, of any kind of fertility. And he was seasoned enough to realize that the connection between them was beyond overwhelming—if he made love to her, the compulsion to bondmate would be unbearable. Becoming lovers would lead to becoming lifemates...and very quickly.

"Stop me," he begged hoarsely, still stroking her nipple. "It's still not too late."

She shook her head, trailing her own fingertips low down his abdomen, twining them in the thick, curling hair between his legs, then sliding them around the tip of his shaft.

"Oh, Anna." He growled, shaking off the last vestiges of his self-control. "Gods above...I tried."

He bent his head and, drawing her nipple between his teeth, nibbled it. He laved it with his tongue until he felt fire chase down his spine. He licked at first one nipple, then the other; blowing a hot breath across the tender skin, he elicited a plaintive cry from her.

"Why would you fight me?" she practically purred.

He shook his head slightly, trailing his tongue in circles about her nipple, and murmured, "Because I'm a thirty-eight-year-old idiot."

"Only smart in the conference room, Lieutenant Daniels?" She giggled uproariously, and he pressed his lips against the skin at the base of her neck, feeling her pulse throb.

"Maybe," he agreed with a soft chuckle. "It's where I first found my nerve with you."

He nuzzled her, suckling at the pulse-point of her neck, hard. Her scent entered his body instantaneously, and the urge to make her his own was so overpowering and strong that he had to work her up beneath him. There was no time to go slow, not now. They might be rescued at any moment; the fantasy-world that they'd created together might crash down around them completely before he could have her.

He lifted off of her, kneeling between her legs and she lay back on the ground, gazing up at him through hooded, sexy eyes. With a quick glance overhead at the late day sky, he estimated that nightfall was eminent.

Rising to his feet, he extended a hand to her. "Come with me, Anna. I have an idea."

She looked up at him in confusion, but he just smiled back at her, drawing her to his side. Without a warning he scooped her into his arms, and she wrapped both legs about him, face-first. His swollen cock bobbed against her abdomen as he carried her toward the open field just a few feet away. Willow grew in places, but mostly it was soft, sun-warmed grass. The perfect meadow for first becoming lovers.

He kept careful hold of her, both of his large hands hitched beneath her thighs, and slowly dropped to the ground until he knelt in the grass that swayed from a slight breeze. Never taking his eyes off of Anna, he lowered her onto her back, and remained kneeling between her thighs. Reaching with one hand, he clasped her hip, with the other he stroked between her legs, immediately feeling the sweet nectar of her arousal. He stroked her harder, his hand trembling as he slid a finger deep inside of her; clutching warmth met his cooler skin and as one they shivered.

Anna leaned back in the grass, her eyes shut with an

expression of pure ecstasy on her face, thick velvet lashes fluttering against her very fair cheeks. Bracing one forearm, he lowered atop of her, still keeping his hips lifted high enough that he could coax and tease the folds of skin between her legs, could plunge deeper with first one finger, then two...now three. She arched her back, and for a moment he settled his hips against hers, levering himself atop of her—although he allowed his fingers to remain inside of her. His breathing grew intense and heavy, her body tensed, and around his fingers he felt a quavering reaction.

Rolling her head back, she tried desperately to pull more of him inside. "Nevin, gods, please." She moaned, bucking her hips up, and his hand fell away. "You, I need *you.*" A scream ripped from her throat; she dug her fingernails into both of his bare shoulders at the precise moment that he plunged within her.

Her hands gripped at his buttocks, squeezing; the smell of earth and dampness and lust filled his nostrils, driving him harder within her—to the very brink. She skimmed both hands along his back, lingering for a moment on the puckered scar of a bullet wound. He gave his head a light shake; they would talk about the battles—all the painful days—later. This one moment was meant for perfection.

Raising his hips, he drew himself out to the very edge and she lifted after him, trying to draw him back inside. She couldn't help whimpering slightly as he kept himself suspended, a wicked grin on his face. "You're a tease," she gasped as he sheathed himself deep within her again.

Wrapping both legs about his waist, she worked him farther in—to the deepest place and his eyes widened, slightly dazed at the pure pleasure and contact.

Over and over, waves of release and need swept over her, and all the while Nevin lasted and lasted. She'd never made love with a man who had his kind of sexual stamina—nor who seemed so able to pull such satisfying release from her.

When she felt the fullest wave of pleasure roll through her body, causing her to moan his name and squirm beneath his heavy frame...he came inside of her. Collapsing, his shoulders covered with a sheen of masculine sweat, he burrowed his face against her neck.

"Ah, Anna Draekus, what have you done to me?" He moaned, nuzzling her playfully.

She stroked her fingertips back and forth over his prickling hair, holding him against her heart. "I think I just unleashed the tiger within you," she finally admitted, giggling.

At first he stiffened within her arms, but then relaxed, a beautiful, masculine laugh rumbling from within his chest. "Just be careful, Anna"—he leaned up on his elbows, staring intently at her—"this tiger has no leash." She reached to touch his face, to let him know that being out of control was okay—but he pressed her palm against his lips. "And I can't promise to be controlled."

"Promise me that you *won't* be."

His smile spread again, a sideways tilt to it as he leaned down to cover her mouth with his own. "That,

Anna Draekus, is probably a guaranteed fact."

Chapter Five

Another day, another sunset, and still no search parties had come. There was only so much you could do, really, to pass the time. At least that's what Nevin told himself as he took Anna within his arms, just one more time. Again and again and again, the lovemaking had been unstoppable. No bounds, no limitations. Thank the gods that they'd had these two days alone, deep within the backcountry, even though he knew that someone would eventually find them. That was a good thing, truly, because you could only subsist on lovemaking and personal energy for just so long.

Anna clung to his body, both of them naked and tangled together, so ready for it. But the lakeshore didn't seem the right setting, not this night; he needed more from her. Hell, they needed more together, something more erotic, more at the very edge of connecting—and that's why he was carting her right into the depths of the barely melted lake.

It would be cold, bracing, but erotic as hell to take her there. For Refarians water was the most arousing element of lovemaking: In the shower, in a steaming pool, even in a frigid lake, and they were driven to near-madness with lust. She thrust her hands through his hair, capturing his mouth with a rough kiss even as he gripped her bare buttocks, steadying her against his own naked body.

She had both legs slung about his waist. Her back was to the lake, her eyes shut as she made love to him with her mouth, murmuring his name over and over. As he stepped into the water, the first splash of the cold liquid sending a jolt through his body, she made a giddy, wild sound in his ear.

"That's going to be damnably cold." She worked to angle herself against his thick cock. If the woman had her way, he'd fuck her blind standing ankle deep in the lake.

"You don't care," he growled back against her ear, taking several deep steps, until, losing his footing, they tumbled together into the chilly water. His body was blazing with heat, burning from the inside out, and a light steam immediately circled them where they stood in the lake. "Besides, I have the gift of energy, remember?"

Already the water that lapped about their waists was warming by multiple degrees. In a matter of moments they would be in a veritable hot pool, the temperature of that small ring about their bodies raised unnaturally.

Anna's heated body first cooled, then immediately began to bathe in a warmth that was totally new for her. The sensation of Nevin's energy spilling into the water about their bodies, the erotic play of it along her skin, almost caused her to lose it right on the spot—especially as he dipped his powerful arms low about her body, drawing her legs about his strong hips once again. "Here," he instructed knowingly, "just float, lean into the water, I have you."

She felt the rounded tip of his erection push against her opening, the mixture of her own wetness and that of the water combining with the silky hardness of his masculine body. "No, hold me!" she cried, scrabbling at him, and he swung her upward until they were pressed chest to chest. "I need to be closer, Nevin. I need to feel all of your body."

He nodded, burying his face against the top of her head, and with a powerful thrust of his hips, pushed inside of her, deep and hard and thrilling. For long moments after he'd penetrated her, they clung to each other, trembling and gasping for the air around them.

"Such a strange place to make love," he admitted with a husky laugh.

"Perfect," she disagreed, showering his warm chest with kisses.

"The bank was so cold."

"And the water..." she barely managed to add as he grasped her hips and brought their bodies to the edge of separation, then drove them back together once again.

For long moments she floated, literally, within his grasp. Unlike their previous times in the past two days, he felt slow, aware of every second that played out between them. Allowing his energy to build about them, he transformed the frigid lake into a bubbling hot tub, the waters churning and pulling at their nude bodies. Nevin shifted his feet on the cool sand beneath them, drawing Anna's legs more tightly about his body. They were at a perfect ninety-degree angle—she floating along her back on the water's surface, he the warrior, the one with the sure-footing, driving into his love once again.

For a brief moment, he gazed up at the full moon; that was the exact moment when he felt their souls brush together. It was the deepest moment for any two Refarians, the one when they could choose—or be compelled—to lifemate. The one when their twin souls would dance together, twining and gyrating into a mystical union.

But he'd not expected it quite this soon. Oh, who was he kidding? He'd known it was likely from the first moment of their crash, his need to meld with her had been that profound.

Floating against him, her eyes flew open. "I felt that."

He bowed his head, giving another gentle, half-thrust. "I did too."

Hidden within his soul, the feather-light brush of her essence pushed closer. His Anna would never be denied, and he'd known that, too, from the very beginning.

His upper lip curled back; he pushed deep inside of her, and sensed thousands of colors merge with his consciousness—it was Anna. Lovely, perfect Anna, melding as one with his own soul.

"Both of us," he cried into the night. "Both of us...one!"

No longer floating within his grasp, she wrapped her

body about his, practically climbing along the length of him. "Yes!" She whooped. "Oh, by the gods, yes, yes, yes."

"Mated," he whispered, pressing his mouth against the top of her head.

With a lighthearted, joyous giggle, she threw both arms about his neck. "Totally, sir!"

The seed inside of her burned a bit; it was different than the other times they'd had sex, relatively few though they were. "Nevin," she murmured as he covered her with his jacket there on the lake's shore. He silenced her with a kiss, and then knelt beside her, stroking a damp tendril of hair back from her cheek.

Naked, he reclined slightly on his side, just watching her through his slanted, sensual eyes, a gorgeous smile on his face. She'd always thought him beautiful before now, but bathed in the moonlight, transformed by their euphoric lovemaking, his handsomeness defied description.

"Nevin," she began again softly, leveling him with a serious look, "I think..." Oh gods above, how to tell the man. She felt her hands shake, but there was no way around it—he had to be told. "There's something you should know."

The glorious smile on his face faded somewhat at her tone. "What is it? You seem upset."

"No!" She sat up, and grabbed hold of both his hands, his jacket slipping down into her lap. "No, I'm not upset.

In fact, it's amazing news...for you. Or maybe for me." She shrugged staring out at the lake. "For both of us," she clarified resolutely.

"Tell me." His words were edged like iron.

"You're not in your maturity." She began to laugh, swinging her gaze toward his face. "I think you're still fertile."

He pressed a hand to his temple, wiping at the sheen of perspiration that had formed between his eyebrows. "This is not amusing—not funny at all."

She cupped her abdomen. "I can feel your essence inside of me now. It's burning, powerful."

He shook his head. "That's not possible," he announced stiffly, turning away from her to stare at the lake.

"I know what I'm feeling."

Turning upon her, he roared, "Look at me, Anna! Look, by All's sake! My outward change doesn't lie!" She swore tears glinted in his black eyes.

"Does it matter?" she asked softly. "Is it bad? Do you not want children?"

He buried his head in both hands, planting both elbows on his knees. "You're confusing me. Is this some strange trick—after what we just shared?" His voice was plaintive and the broken sound of it tore at her heart.

She sidled up next to him, kneeling, and placed both hands on his shoulders. "Nevin," she whispered gently, "I can only tell you what I feel."

"You wouldn't know...would you?" he added the last in a soft, almost hopeful voice.

"Well, from what I'm told, that burning sensation only comes when a Refarian male is at the height of his fertility."

He shook his head, closing his eyes. "That is true. Totally and completely true."

Anna edged around until she met his gaze, saw the powerful emotion on Nevin's face. Oh, he wanted it to be true all right, so much so that it was obvious he didn't even dare hope. "If it's true," she said gently, "then you know what it means."

He squeezed his eyes shut. "We can't possibly have done so."

She threw her arms about his neck. "You might have just given me a child."

"All this need, this urgent hunger," he whispered in her ear, "it's you, Anna. You brought me back into my season somehow. Just being so near you for these past few days."

"Do you really think that kind of thing is impossible? Maybe it was just different for you, your change. Maybe your hair silvered, but"—she ran her hands sensually down his chest—"but your body never changed."

"Oh it changed all right." He gasped, his lungs pulling at the night air around them. "You've awakened me like I've never known." He clasped her face between his palms, staring into her eyes for a long, hungry moment, literally trying to take her inside of himself somehow. "You've changed me, Anna—in a very short period of time."

Pressing her forehead against his, she whispered, "You said something about the meeting room. That you first noticed me then. Was it when I had to come explain about the Madjin?"

He held her close against his chest, feeling the rapid pounding of her heart against his own. She needed to know the truth. "No, Anna. That was just the first time I let myself show you that I'd been noticing you for a very, very long time."

She jerked backward, her dark eyes wide like the moon above them both. "Okay, you did get some kind of...look, or something, that day! I knew it."

He laughed, stroking his hand down the length of her silky hair. "It was all that talk about your energy. It turned me on, completely."

She scowled at him playfully. "You could have done something about it."

"I wish I'd known how. I tried, I supposed, that day in the conference room"—he frowned—"I just didn't know how to make you notice me."

"I've noticed you for years, Nevin." She cupped his cheek significantly. "And now look what's happened."

His eyes grew hooded and dangerous looking. "We're mated. For life." Inside of her soul, she felt a demanding pull, a surge of ownership from Nevin's soul against her own.

"When you finally get down to it, you don't waste any time, do you?" She laughed, adding, "Sir."

He lay back onto the ground beneath them, staring up at the night sky with a deeply serene expression. "I expect you to add a salute with that, Lieutenant Draekus."

She lay down against him, resting her head over his heart. "Salute this," she teased, sliding her hand between his legs.

One black eyebrow cocked upward. "You may not get a return salute from that department, at least not for a few more minutes."

"I can wait. We have forever now—no matter what happens, we're bonded together."

Nevin smiled, but inside he felt a terrible wave of dread. Having mated and bonded themselves to each other was one thing while they were here in the wilderness—but how would they possibly handle such an awkward proposition once back on base? He was still her commanding officer, and nothing about that problem had been resolved.

With a slight shake of his head, he drew Anna much closer within his arms, needing to feel her warmth, her tenderness. "Yes, we do have forever," he promised. Inside his heart, however, he didn't feel quite so sure.

Chapter Six

A hard object kept bumping into her thigh. Repeatedly. But sleep was so cozy, what with the early morning sun warming their bodies, that she didn't mind. She just rolled closer to Nevin, nestling against his uniform-clad chest, and pulled his jacket over them both.

"Anna." It was the voice of her twin sister.

"Go away. I'm still sleeping," she murmured drowsily.

Sudden cold covered her half-bare body as the jacket ripped away; Nevin bolted upright beside her, and together they discovered Anika and a full rescue party gaping at them.

"Oh, *medshki*," Anna muttered, her gaze sliding first to Nevin's half-buttoned, disheveled uniform, then to her own bare legs, and finally back to her twin's eager face. Anna pulled frantically at the uniform jacket, covering herself.

Anika issued a quiet command to the rest of the party, and they immediately moved away toward the lake, giving the three of them privacy.

Nevin staggered to his feet, smoothing out his

uniform. "Lieutenant Draekus," he said, addressing her twin sister. "Thank you for your diligence in finding us."

Anika inclined her head slightly. "My apologies, sir, that it took so long." Then, much to Anna's dismay, her sister's gaze slid between them meaningfully. "I trust you fared well during this incident?"

Nevin ran an anxious hand over his new growth of beard, blushing. "We are well, Lieutenant."

Anna remained on the ground, watching the interchange, and wondered why Nevin didn't just announce the news of their lifemating. This was her own twin sister, after all, the only other person on the planet that she shared an intense connection with.

But Nevin said nothing—didn't so much as comment on their compromising position—while the rescue party gathered their meager belongings from beside the lake.

Anika glanced at her, confusion obvious, but Anna gave her head a light shake. It would be up to Nevin how they handled this; as much as it irritated her, she did understand that he would be cautious about sharing their news. Most likely they would have to return to base first, and then the news would become common knowledge.

Anika extended a hand to her, grinning conspiratorially. "Come now, sis, let's go board the craft. I have a warm breakfast waiting for you both. You can tell me all about"—Anika cut her eyes sideways subtly—"your adventures."

Nevin sat impatiently in the medical area, ruing like hell his actions of the past hours. Returning to the compound had disconcerted him—especially his commander's concern about their well-being. There'd been one key moment when he should have confessed everything to their commander, Jared Bennett, let him know the truth about Anna and their lifebonding. But that moment had slid past, and he'd kept his mouth shut. Afterward Anna had gazed at him with such raw pain in her gorgeous black eyes that he'd been rendered speechless.

"You don't intend to have anyone know," she'd said, clutching at his arm.

Waving her to the far corner of the main room, he'd whispered, "Not now, Anna. Give it time."

"We can't keep this secret—you do know that."

He'd given her a stern look. "Lieutenant, our first duties are within this military. Not to each other."

Mouth agape, she'd backed away from him, saying nothing.

"Anna!" he'd called, but she had kept on walking.

Shortly after that, she vacated the main compound, and he'd not seen her since. When it became apparent that she wasn't returning, he finally decided to visit his personal doctor down on the base. The least he could do was learn the truth about the situation between he and Anna—the biological truth, that was.

The doctor appeared in the waiting room. "Lieutenant Daniels," he said with a pleasant smile, "please come with me."

Nevin rolled down his shirt sleeve, arm aching from the blood sample the doctor had just drawn. "So you'll be able to tell me today?" he asked the doctor who had already injected his sample into the diagnostic computer.

"I'll be able to tell you within moments—just have to let the data upload."

Nevin raked both hands through his hair. "I don't get it," he complained, "Look at me—silver-haired and totally mature by every outward sign. And yet you're saying I might still be fertile?"

"It's not common, but it does happen on rare occasions," the man explained, studying the computer screen. Nevin's heart began to pound; if he was still fertile, that could mean... "Of course, if you aren't actually mature, then you need to be thinking about any unprotected sex you might have had recently."

Inwardly, Nevin groaned. Unprotected sex? Oh, yes indeed he'd had it; he should have taken precautions it now seemed, but more than that, he should have done a better job of protecting his heart too.

The computer screen changed hue, a data trail scrolling downward, and the doctor let out a whistle. "Good grief, Lieutenant, you're not just fertile—you're as fertile as a *gnangat'ai* in springtime."

"Wh-what?" Nevin stammered.

The doctor spun to face him, grinning like a school boy. "You're what we deem 'dynamically fertile', sir. Congratulations. You must be having a splendid time of it."

Nevin blushed painfully. "I don't understand."

"The rare Refarian male makes a change—gets the silver hair like you've got there—but his body enters a sort of sexual hyper-zone. His drives intensify keenly, his fertility ratio goes off the charts...and it lasts for years. If you've been making love to any women lately...?"

"Just one," Nevin admitted, throat dry as he thought of Anna. Gods, if he'd gotten her pregnant, there'd be no hiding their lifebonding.

"Well, if you coupled with her more than once, you might not be looking at just one pregnancy, but a second laid down on top of that one. Possibly a third."

"Doctor, are you trying to give me fucking heart failure?" Nevin barked.

"I'm trying to explain the situation to you, young man. You are a fertility powerhouse right now—and if you've been spreading your seed around beyond that one woman, you may need to figure out just how many children you've sired."

"You're my doctor, you should have warned me about this. I saw you after my hair went silver."

The doctor shook his head. "And you were no longer fertile. Something brought this on."

"Something—or someone?" Nevin thought of the absolute mating *frenzy* that Anna had put him in.

"Yes, high fertility like this can be induced by a particular partner. It's nature's way, you know, how newly mature men become so randy. Every now and then, too, it drives the male back into fertility. You might even go black-headed again," the doctor volunteered with a jocular laugh.

Nevin shot a look at himself in the sink mirror, and imagined himself with dark, unsilvered hair once again. Then he flinched, realizing that he might have seeded several babies inside of Anna. "I need to find that woman," he said, still studying himself in the mirror.

"She's not just any woman, now is she, Lieutenant Daniels?"

He grinned at the wizened doctor. "No, doctor," he admitted with a grin, "she's my lifemate."

When Nevin returned to the lodge, Anna was nowhere to be found, and he learned from her twin sister that she'd been working with several soldiers down at Base Ten. It felt as if she would never return, and although he retreated to the meeting room to study schematics and some battle strategies, he couldn't bring his mind to focus. All he could think of was Anna being pregnant— maybe even with multiple babies. As much as he yearned for a family with her, it was the last thing either of them had really imagined.

When nightfall came, he made an appearance at dinner, positioning himself at the table with Jared and

Kelsey. He could only hope that Anna's hurt and anger from his earlier behavior wouldn't keep her gone all night. He'd been cruel, treating her dismissively with their king, and she hadn't deserved any of it.

Of course she wanted to share quarters with him— and of course she wanted the world to know. As the day had worn on, he'd realized what a ridiculous fool he'd been to even imagine that they could hide the true nature of their relationship, the depth of their lifebonding, from those around them.

Beside him, Jared cleared his throat, explaining that he'd voiced some polite question three times now without a reply. Nevin blinked back at him, feeling dazed.

He placed his right fist over his heart, and bowed deeply. "Apologies, my lord," he said, feeling ashamed to have shown such dishonor to his king and commander.

"Rise, Lieutenant," Jared told him impatiently. Nevin knew all too well that the king had little patience for his deeply held traditions, but he would as soon have resigned his position than treat his commander any differently.

Again, Jared intruded on his thoughts. *"N'Vsai,* are you feeling all right?" Only then did he realize he was still frozen, one hand over his heart, bowing deeply. With a stiff gesture, he sat up straight in the chair.

"No, my lord, I am feeling quite...unlike myself."

"The past few days took a toll on you, I am certain," Jared agreed.

Kelsey gazed at him in concern. "Perhaps you should

go to the medical area?"

"No!" He shook his head, softening his tone. "No, my lady, I have already been."

"It wouldn't hurt you to go back," she offered, clearly wondering why he'd been so adamant.

Pressing both hands to his temples, he decided that there was no moment like the present; sucking in a fortifying breath he whispered, "I have much to confess."

Nevin tossed back a shot of whiskey that his king had poured for him. "Well, congratulations are definitely in order," Jared had thundered joyously. Nevin wished he could share his king's good humor.

"Sir, you don't seem to understand—I have faltered to the worst possible extent with her. There may well be nothing to celebrate," he admitted miserably, draining the rest of the whiskey.

Jared wasted no time, and hit him again; Nevin wasted no time, either, and drained the glass dry with one gulp. He saw Jared's black eyes sparkle with amusement.

Nevin turned to him, feeling fuzzy and warm and tossed both hands in the air. "I know! I know! It doesn't seem at all like me, does it?" he half-slurred. "She's changed me, Jared, that's why. She did something to me, Kelsey." He plunked his glass back down on the table, feeling very cozy with his king and queen. It felt nice to call them by their first names.

He saw them exchange a look, stifling smiles, the both of them. "Go on, it's all right. Laugh. I'm sure this is pretty amusing, isn't it?"

Jared slipped an arm about his shoulder. "*N'Vsai*, it's only amusing because in the past months my wife and I have known just how falling in love can dismantle you. Completely. It strikes me that Anna has had quite the time taking you apart, piece by piece."

"She's pregnant," Nevin blurted, reaching for the bottle of whiskey himself.

He didn't have to look at the royal pair to see the confusion in their faces. "Yes, indeed, it seems that"—he thunked a fist against his chest proudly—"that I'm actually fertile as the day is long. Nobody knew it. Nobody told me, so hell no, we didn't take a single precaution. The doc says she might have a few babes inside of her already. A *few*."

Nevin paused only long enough to drain yet another glass filled with Scotch, holding his verbal place in the conversation by keeping one hand extended. "And she has no idea," he gulped, slamming the glass down once again. Only this time Jared slid it out of his reach, and Kelsey took the bottle back into the kitchen.

"You need to slow down there, Nevin." Jared propped both hands behind his head, tilting backward in his chair. "Otherwise, you and your lovely new lifemate will have one hell of a time when she returns. You don't want to unload all of this upon her without warning."

"She's not coming back, sir. That's what I'm telling

you—I totally blew it with her this morning. She thinks I'm ashamed for the camp to know we're together."

"Are you?"

"Absolutely not—but I *am* ashamed of my poor judgment. I completely failed you, my lord." Nevin buried his head within his hands miserably. "I am her superior officer; I knew better..."

"There are no directives within our military structure that forbid lifemating."

"None that are spelled out." Nevin slapped a fist against the table. "But I feel the weight of my position, my lord." He turned in his chair, meeting Jared's gaze soberly. "I have failed you. If you wish for my resignation, you shall have it."

Jared frowned, tilting his head sideways. "You have always confused me, Nevin. Your intensity, your seriousness. Now, more than ever. Anna will make a splendid lifemate for you. What is your real concern?"

Nevin stared into his king's eyes, and for the very first time understood his real fears about loving Anna. "I have no control with her, not even an ounce of it."

His queen, returning from the kitchen, began to laugh. "Nevin, you aren't supposed to have control with your mate. That's the whole point."

"But it's terrifying," he admitted, bowing his head solemnly.

"That," Jared agreed with a laugh of his own, "is also the point. And if I were you, I'd go to her quickly—at least based on my own experience."

"You are certain, my lord?" Nevin searched his king's face and saw nothing but support and genuine happiness.

"With our blessing." Jared rose from his seat, carrying his plate with him. "But don't blurt out the part about the babies until you've had the chance to truly make up. Just a piece of advice from my marital career so far."

Nevin took the connecting hallways and elevator, but apparently his lifemate had taken the trail outside, heading back up to the lodge. In exasperation, he exited the lower area of the base, hit the trail and began hiking up the mountain at an aggressive rate. The remaining snow along the mountain path was packed, so there wasn't any making out her boot prints; when he didn't reach her, he punched at his communicator angrily. "I need the location of Lieutenant Anna Draekus," he commanded.

He expected her to answer, but the only reply he got was that she'd left the base around approximately fifteen minutes earlier—and this was not new intel.

Nothing at all came over the comm from his lifemate. "I'm still her commanding officer, and I'll be damned if she won't answer me," he muttered, the former glow from the whiskey morphing into irritability.

"Lieutenant Anna Draekus, your position please?" he called into the comm, but she didn't answer at all.

Damn it, all he wanted was to find his mate, to make up with her, to lay with her, to tell her the deepest secrets of his heart. And he wanted all of that—every last bit of it—right now. Not later, not another day, but now.

Sinking to the ground, he calculated his position in regards to love; he and Anna were forever tied together by the bond that they'd formed. However, she could choose to shut him out forever—even though he had to admit it didn't seem much like her personality. Still, the thought of never holding her again stabbed at his most primal, base instincts. He tossed back his head and howled his need for her, giving in to the dizzying lusts that kept pummeling through his body.

No answer came from the woods, not that he expected it would. He stared upward at the moon and released a melancholy, plaintive cry for her...still no sound in return. Would she even know his call if she heard it? It was personal, intimate, memorized over time between lovers.

Personal, like their energy, he thought, his mood instantly brightening. Oh, yes, he had a brilliant idea of how to win Anna back. Opening his palm, he allowed a glowing sphere of his power to form until it swirled beneath his two hands. Working it upward toward his lips, he leaned forward and whispered her name into the fiery orb. Over and over, he whispered "Anna... Anna..." Infusing his energy with all the love he felt for her. Then, raising his hands high, he released the energy into the night woods and watched as it shot up the dark mountainside, seeking her out like his own personal missile.

Anna stood on the deck of the main lodge, staring at the stars overhead. It was a perfectly clear night that seemed *perfectly* designed to illuminate her heartbreak. From deep within the woods below she'd almost imagined the sound of Nevin's cry for her, but she knew her heart was only imagining what it wanted to hear.

The sound came again, more plaintive, desperate. Needy. She leaned over the railing, listening intently; silence was her only answer.

Tears stung her eyes, blurring her vision, and she blinked at them hopelessly. Of course Nevin wouldn't lay claim to their bond now that they were back in the compound. Of course he would return to the man she'd always known before, so controlled and unemotional. The only surprise at all was that Anna hadn't anticipated his behavior.

Lifting a hand to wipe away her tears, she spotted an eerie light down below the deck. The woods glowed unnaturally, as if some powerful energized being were moving through the area. Anna tensed, clutching at the railing, and tried to get a better view. *Perhaps it's our commander, moving through the woods in his natural form,* she thought. *Yes, that has to be it.*

She shuddered. *Or maybe it's one of our enemies, probing us.*

Reaching carefully, she found her pulse pistol holstered at her hip. Her fingers twitched, but she didn't make a move for fear that she'd alert this being—whoever it was—to her presence.

The glowing intensified, moving up the mountain rapidly—and aiming right for her. "Anna," she heard whispered through the dense trees. "Anna..."

Before she could blink, the orb of brilliant energy made a beeline for her, seeking her out with intense purpose. "Anna," came Nevin's whisper again, from deep within the energy sphere. His power was so blinding, she could barely keep her eyes open.

She sensed his invitation, his pure desire to have her touch this part of himself. Glancing all about them, she searched for him. "Where are you?" she muttered aloud, her gaze sweeping the side of the main lodge.

"Right here," came his throaty, emotional reply from just behind her. She jolted, and he caught her from behind, clasping her shoulders with firm, staying hands.

"Your energy?" She squinted, trying to gaze at it in the pure darkness. Up close like this, it was absolutely blinding.

"It was the only way I could think to find you."

"You sent it after me? Like a homing beacon?"

He pressed his lips against the top of her head, blowing out a heavy breath. "You're my lifemate. My energy reacts to that, feels it. But that wasn't the only thing." He wrapped his muscular arms about her waist, pinning her against him. "I wanted to reveal my energy to you...intimately. Sensually, not like the other times when we were stranded. This is the most vulnerable part of me."

Tears brimmed in her eyes anew. From the very

beginning between them, their respective energies had been a staging area, a line neither would cross willingly.

She forced her eyes open, leaning back against his chest. "How could All have ever made something so incredibly beautiful?" she whispered.

"Touch it."

"I-I can't."

"I would never hurt you, Anna," he promised, pressing his lips against her ear. "Not intentionally. That I hurt you earlier, well, it's torn me up inside. But with my touch? With my energy? No, I will never hurt you. *Never.*"

Extending both hands, she placed her palms around the undulating sphere; at that precise moment, her lifemate's very energy shot deep within her, setting her entire body afire. She began to quaver, feeling her legs grow wobbly, but he anchored her against his chest. After a moment, she began to giggle, feeling light-headed and drunk.

"You just got me high!" She turned in his arms until her cheek rested against his massive chest.

"I'm a little drunk," he admitted shyly, "so that just evens the odds."

She pulled back, gazing up into his dark eyes. For a minute, she swore that his hair seemed a little darker too. "Why did you get drunk?"

With a shake of his head, he stroked her hair, quiet for long moments. "I was terrified, Anna. Of you, of this change in me, of our lifemating...but mostly of you."

"I don't understand. We're fantastic together, so beautiful, so amazing—"

"Because I have no control when it comes to you."

Anna snorted. "It's about damn time you lost control, *N'Vsai*. I'm just honored that it happened with me."

His mouth tilted upward in a sideways smile. "Does this mean that you forgive me? For being a stupid *stratkai*?"

Anna leaned up onto her tiptoes, planting a full, wet kiss squarely on his cheek. "If you're planning to tell Jared our news."

Nevin's gorgeous smile widened. "I've already done that. And then some, I'm afraid."

"I don't think I want to know what that means."

He slid his arm about her shoulder, walking her toward the door that led to the lodge interior. "Well, sweet Anna, there's a little something I need to tell you about visiting the doctor earlier today."

And then he tossed his head back and laughed more deeply than she'd ever heard him do. A strange feeling began deep within her belly at the sound of it, almost like a quiet answer. A knowing answer.

She stopped in her tracks. "I was right—wasn't I? About the way it felt the last time we made love?"

He slid a large palm over her belly. "The doctor described my condition as 'dynamically fertile'. He also let me know that it was in reaction to you, Anna. You."

She covered his hand against her stomach. "So does

this mean I'm pregnant? Already?"

Her lifemate had the gall to look proud of himself, cocky even, as he thrust his chest out. "I believe you said of men my age that we—what was it now? 'Rut like fucking stallions'?"

"*What* did the doctor *say*?"

Nevin's dark eyes gleamed. "That you are likely carrying our child."

She thrust her arms about his neck, squealing. "I told you. I absolutely told you, didn't I?"

"And he also said that we can't make love without some kind of protection for a while, or there will be more and more babies."

She pulled out of his arms, studying him. "You're afraid that I'm already pregnant with multiples." He bowed his head, but said nothing. "Nevin, it only burned inside of me that one time. You don't need to worry."

"Can you live with this? A man like me?" He cast a shy look up at her. "One with these kinds of raging needs and desires...who might give you many babies, whether intentional or not?"

She gaped at him, then slugged him lightly in the chest. "You, sir, are unbelievable. First you worried that you couldn't give me children, now you worry that you'll give me too many? I love you, Nevin. Do you hear that? Children or no children, age gap or not, I love you. Nothing can alter that."

His arms closed about her, and he drew her into an almost-suffocating embrace. "I love you too. Gods, it's insanity the way this has happened, but it's right. Deeply right, and I know it."

She closed her eyes and stood, just feeling the warmth of him, until a thought occurred to her. "So," she asked with a giggle, "did you tell Commander Bennett about the rutting like a stallion part? Or did you leave that much out of our story?"

He swatted her bottom playfully. "Let's go to bed, Lieutenant. I'll share all my secrets there."

About the Author

To learn more about Deidre Knight, please visit www.deidreknight.com. Send an email to Deidre Knight at Deidre@Deidreknight.com or join her Yahoo! group to join in the fun with other readers as well as Deidre! http://groups.yahoo.com/group/DeidreKnight

An immortal soldier defies the ancient Gods he serves and puts his existence and the world at risk when he saves the life of the mortal woman he swore to kill.

Immortal Protector
© *2007 Ursula Bauer*

Gideon Sinclair, an immortal, shape-shifting soldier, defies the ancient gods he serves, risking his existence and the future of the mortal world, when he saves the life of the woman he was sworn to kill: Dr. Megan Carter. For centuries he's fought for justice and balance in the eternal struggle between good and evil. Gideon challenges destiny and the forces aligning against her, but when Meg becomes more than a mission, will he be able to accept the healing love she offers or will their enemies and the demons of his past be their undoing?

Meg's accidental contact with an artifact sacred to the Goddess Isis thrusts her into the midst of a centuries old battle between two rival gods, and makes her the target of a crazed magician bent on unlocking the secrets of immortality. With nowhere to turn and no one to trust, she puts her life in the hands of the lethal, enigmatic Gideon, and is drawn into his dark world. She can't resist the passionate desire he stirs, but will she pay the ultimate price when she falls for a man who no longer has a heart?

Available now in ebook and print from Samhain Publishing.

Enjoy the following excerpt from Immortal Protector…

Meg was out of the car and moving, any thoughts of her own safety gone from her mind. Gideon started to come round as she ran up her walk. The demon moved slower, as if in pain. She trampled the pansies and pulled the sword from the marigolds. The creature took note of her, snorted, and kept walking towards the immortal.

Gideon got to his knees, saw the demon coming down with a vicious swing, and lurched to the side. He rolled into the spill and came up on his feet just in time to sidestep another strike. This close Meg could see the other wounds. His shirt was sliced in a few spots, and blood poured freely. His cheekbone was bruised, and he was favoring his right leg.

The blade felt incredibly light in her hands. Her heart rammed hard against her ribs. She couldn't breathe. She couldn't move. But she managed. She put one foot in front of the other, and reached him just before the demon.

"Run. Meg. Run," he ground out between clenched teeth. He grabbed the sword from her and lunged.

Meg stepped clear and started to back away as the two engaged in a series of traded strikes. The demon pivoted on the last salvo, changed gears, and made a run towards her. Before it could connect, Gideon leapt in between them, blade gripped with both hands, poised up in a defensive position. The creature's sword connected, and Gideon's sword severed the curved blade in two. A brilliant burst of light accompanied the sheering of steel, and the demon lurched back with an ungodly hiss.

Gideon pressed his advantage, taking a series of offensive strikes that connected more than they missed. He fought the creature back into the little house and disappeared around the corner of the vestibule. Meg knew she should go back to the car, every part of her sane mind told her to run away, but instead, she ran into the house, following her immortal. She didn't know the rules, didn't know the physiology of an immortal, but Gideon was a mess. She dearly hoped immortals couldn't be killed. But if they couldn't, why would he have so many weapons?

She hit her living room and froze in her tracks. Red blood and yellow gore covered her walls. Ash littered her furniture. What was left of it, at least. Her books were out of the built-in shelves and scattered in piles. Everything remotely breakable was in pieces. Even the floorboards fell victim. They were torn down to the joists in several spots. Gideon and the creature fought in her kitchen. She moved fully into the room and saw them as they traded blows. The demon had some kind of dagger now, but it was no match for Gideon's superior weapon.

Meg worried a creature like that would fight dirtier, have more tricks. And she worried about Gideon. He was hurt, bad, and showing signs of fatigue. Meg swallowed the panic threatening to consume her and walked into her kitchen. Her kitchen, her house, her immortal soldier. He needed an advantage. He needed help. He needed her.

She was a mortal, but she wasn't an idiot. However mythical the creature in her kitchen, it still had the same rise and fall of the thoracic region, demonstrating it still had to breathe. The first thing they taught in emergency responder class was to clear the airway. No airway, everything else was a wash. The exposed nasal passage presented an excellent point of entry. As calmly as she might grab a mug from the bakers rack near the south facing window and pour herself morning coffee, she pulled the fire extinguisher from the wall holder, moved into position, and opened up on the face of the demon.

The white foam shot out in a single stream and she angled it towards the wide nose holes. It was sucking wind already from the fight and couldn't stop from inhaling the chemical antidote for fire. The foam was designed to expand on contact and that's exactly what it did. The demon's features seized, it grabbed for its throat and lurched back, coughing and choking. It banged into her stove and pushed it through the dry wall. Gideon used the momentary diversion and drove his sword through its exposed flank. As he pulled back his blade, a brilliant white light flared through the kitchen, its epicenter the demon's rapidly disintegrating body. Then, a second later, everything returned to normal. All that remained was the destruction and a scattering of dark gray ash.

Gideon lowered his sword and it vanished. He staggered back hard into her refrigerator, braced his hands on his knees and slid to the floor. He looked up at her, a mixture of confusion, and something she couldn't quite identify in his eyes. Then his visage shifted. His lips formed a hard frown, and his burning coal black eyes pinned her with an incendiary glare. "I told you to...wait...in...the...car."

"Save the thanks." She found herself finally able to breathe now that he was safe. Now that they were safe. "I don't know much about immortals, but I'm willing to bet you could use a few Band-Aids right now. I'll be right back with my med kit."

Gideon wiped the sweat and blood from his forehead. His lungs burned from breathing in all the ash and from the taxing battle. He couldn't seem to get enough air. He briefly considered moving and started to push up to a standing position, but his body screamed in pain, so he decided instead to sit and wait for the doc. He was pissed at her for risking her pretty little neck, and he was damned impressed that she'd wade into battle with demons without a second thought. She was a red-headed Valkyrie, and a genius. Spraying the Keeper in the face with the extinguisher gave Gideon the edge he'd desperately needed to turn the battle. Even without the sword, the Keeper was an ass kicker. Only one thing bothered him. The Keeper shouldn't have died. Not from a flank wound.

Gideon had skewered the thing to help immobilize it, choosing the sweet spot: the nexus points of nerves that clustered on either flank of a demon. The thing's hands blocked the neck, preventing beheading, but a shot to the sweet spot would result in momentary paralysis, giving him a chance to fell a killing blow. Except the strike finished the thing as effectively as beheading. It made no sense. And things that made no sense bothered him.

He heard Meg's approach as she muttered curses to herself. She carried a little black bag, like something a country doctor might have. She scowled at him and knelt by his side.

"Take your jacket off, and your shirt."

He smiled and shrugged out of his leathers. "What ever you say, Doc."

"Don't get too excited. This is a professional visit, not a social call."

The T-shirt was shredded and useless to him, so he pulled the tatters from his body. Meg might think this was a professional visit, but, judging by the way her pupils dilated and she licked her lips with that delicate pink tongue, he'd bet she was enjoying the view anyway. He felt a sharp stab of masculine pride. The doc liked him. He started grinning like an idiot, even though he felt like hell. "I have a small kit in the jacket pocket. I heal fast. That will help me heal faster if it's applied to the wounds."

Wordlessly, she grabbed the jacket, removed the small, hard-shelled kit and opened it up. "Which one?"

"The cobalt-blue bottle."

She opened it and sniffed, then wrinkled her nose. "It smells like raw sewage. What's it made of?"

"This and that."

"Let's start with some cleaning. We can use this later."

She sealed it up, opened her own bag, and set up shop.

Gideon watched as she ripped the seal off a small plastic tray, dropped in several gauze pads, and filled the tray with saline. Her movements were smooth, practiced, economical. He found himself both dreading and longing for her touch.

"This may hurt." Much to his disappointment, she donned a pair of latex gloves. "I want to clean the wound on your head first."

She repositioned, leaning over him so she could better assess the wound. It gave him a spectacular view of her breasts and brought her body so close she ignited him with a slow, dangerous flame. She touched his forehead lightly, and her lips formed a slight, delectable pout. "The blood flow appears to have stopped. Amazing."

If he straightened just a bit, moved an inch or so to the right, he could capture those juicy lips and kiss away any frowns. "You have no idea."

She changed gears and moved back on her heels so she could give his chest and abdomen a better look. Her hand feathered across his bare skin and he shivered at her touch.

The corners of her lips tilted up. "You're ticklish?"

"What can I say, Doc. You have the touch."

She colored slightly and turned away, keeping her eyes solidly focused on his naked torso. He had to suppress the urge to grab her and roll her beneath him. He had a vivid image of how she would look, how she would feel. He felt himself start to harden and pushed away the tantalizing thoughts of her soft body, pliable and hot beneath his own. She'd taste sweet as cotton candy, melt in the mouth sweet. He knew it. He craved it.

LaVergne, TN USA
09 August 2010
192616LV00003B/52/P